PADDINGTON™

A Day Out

WANTED ON VOYAGE

Written by Karen Jamieson

Collins

What does Paddington see on his day out?

A red shop.

A red coat.

A black bird.

A black taxi.

A yellow boat.

A yellow car.

A green park.

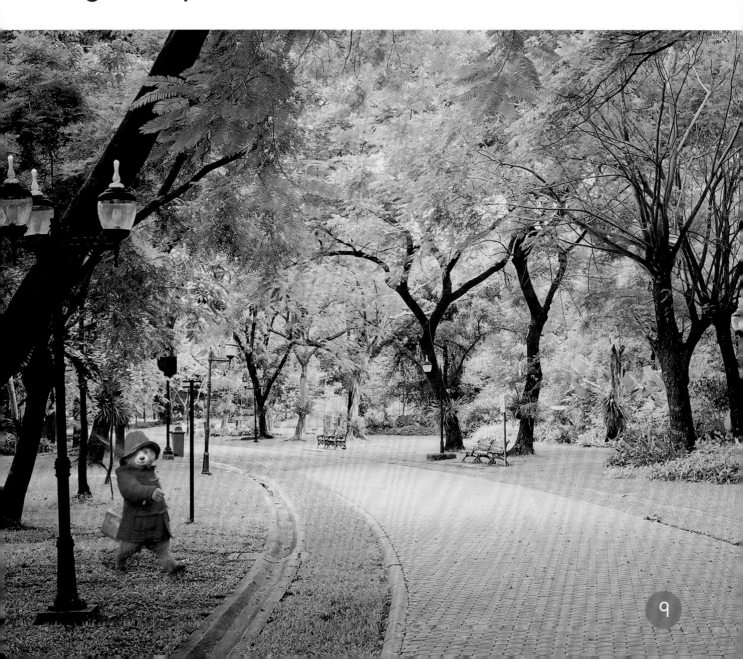

A green bike.

A blue bridge.

11

Blue sky!

A good day out!

Colours

red

black

yellow

green

blue

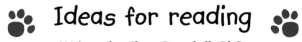

Ideas for reading

Written by Clare Dowdall, PhD
Lecturer and Primary Literacy Consultant

Reading objectives:
- read and understand simple sentences
- use phonic knowledge to decode regular words and read them aloud accurately
- read some common irregular words
- demonstrate understanding when talking with others about what they have read

Communication and language objectives:
- express themselves effectively, showing awareness of listeners' needs

- use past, present and future forms accurately when talking about events that have happened

Curriculum links: Understanding the world – The world; Expressive arts and development – Exploring and using media and materials; Being imaginative; Literacy – Writing

Resources: coloured toys and items for children to find; display table, card and paints or pens for colour labels

Word count: 46

Build a context for reading

- Read the title together. Model how to use phonic knowledge to sound out regular words.
- Ask children to explain what they think a day out is, and to recount what they like to do on a day out.
- Ask children to look carefully at the picture on the front cover. Help them to use new vocabulary to describe what they can see.
- Read the blurb to children: *What does Paddington see on his day out?* Challenge children to predict what Paddington will see on his day out in the big city.

Understand and apply reading strategies

- Turn to pp2–3. Read the question again: *What does Paddington see on his day out?* Ask children to read the answer with you: *A red shop.*
- Ask children to predict something else that Paddington may see in the big city that is red, then turn the page to find out what he did see. Help children to read the sentence together: *A red coat.*

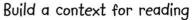